Treasured Tales

Snow White

p

Long, long ago, in a faraway land, there lived a king and queen who had a beautiful baby girl. Her lips were as red as cherries, her hair as black as coal, and her skin as white as snow—her name was Snow White.

Sadly, the queen died, and years later the king married again. The new queen was very beautiful, but also evil, cruel, and vain. She had a magic mirror, and every day she looked into it and asked, "Mirror, mirror on the wall, who is the fairest one of all?"

And every day, the mirror replied, "You, O Queen, are the fairest!"

Time passed, and every year Snow White grew more beautiful. The queen became increasingly jealous of her stepdaughter.

One day, the magic mirror gave the queen a different answer to her question. "Snow White is the fairest one of all!" it replied.

The queen was furious. She ordered her huntsman to take Snow White deep into the forest and kill her.

But the huntsman couldn't bear to harm Snow White. "Run away!" he told her. "Run away and never come back, or the queen will kill us both!" Snow White fled deep into the forest.

As Snow White rushed through the trees she came upon a tiny cottage. She knocked at the door and then went in—the house was empty. There she found a tiny table with seven tiny chairs. Upstairs there were seven little beds. Exhausted, she lay down across them and fell asleep.

Many hours later, Snow White woke to see seven little faces peering at her. The dwarfs, who worked in a diamond mine, had returned home and wanted to know who the pretty young girl was.

Snow White told them her story and why she had to run away. They all sat around her and listened to her tale.

When she had finished, the eldest dwarf said, "If you will look after our house for us, we will keep you safe. But please don't let anyone into the cottage while we are at work!"

The next morning, when the wicked queen asked the mirror her usual question, she was horrified when it answered, "The fairest is Snow White, gentle and good. She lives in a cottage, deep in the wood!"

The queen was furious; she had been tricked. She magically disguised herself as an old peddler and set off into the wood to seek out Snow White and kill the girl herself.

That afternoon, Snow White heard a tap-tapping at the window. She looked out and saw an old woman with a basket full of bright ribbons and laces.

"Pretty things for sale," cackled the old woman.

Snow White remembered the dwarfs' warning. But the ribbons and laces were so lovely, and the woman seemed so harmless, that she let her in.

"Try this lace in your dress, my dear," said the old woman. Snow White happily let the woman thread the new lace. But the lace was pulled so tight that Snow White fainted.

Certain that at last she had killed her stepdaughter, the queen raced through the forest, back to her castle, laughing evilly.

That evening, when the dwarfs returned home, they were shocked to discover Snow White lying lifeless on the floor. They loosened the laces on her dress so she could breathe and made her promise again not to let any strangers in when they were at work.

The next day, when the mirror told the queen that Snow White was still alive, she was livid and vowed to kill her once and for all. She disguised herself and went back to the cottage.

This time the old woman took with her a basket of lovely red apples. She had poisoned the biggest, reddest one of all. She knocked on the door and called out, "Juicy red apples for sale."

The apples looked so delicious that Snow White just had to buy one. She opened the door and let the old woman in. "My, what pretty, rosy cheeks you have, dear," said the woman, "the very color of my apples. Here, take a bite and see how good they are." She handed Snow White the biggest one....

Snow White took a big bite and fell to the floor—dead. The old woman fled into the forest, happy at last.

This time, the dwarfs could not bring Snow White back to life. Overcome with grief, they placed her gently in a glass coffin and carried it to a quiet clearing in the forest. And there they sat, keeping watch over their beloved Snow White.

One day, a handsome young prince came riding through the forest and saw the beautiful young girl in the glass coffin. He fell in love with her at once and begged the dwarfs to let him take her back to his castle.

At first the dwarfs refused, but when they saw how much the prince loved their Snow White, they agreed.

As the prince lifted the coffin to carry it away, he stumbled, and the piece of poisoned apple fell from Snow White's mouth, where it had been lodged all this time. Snow White's eyes fluttered open, and she looked up and saw the handsome young man.

"Where am I?" she asked him in a bewildered voice. "Who are you?"

"I am your prince," he said. "And you are safe with me now. Please marry me and come to live in my castle!" He leaned forward and kissed her cheek.

"Oh, yes, sweet prince," cried Snow White. "Of course I will."

The next day, the magic mirror told the wicked queen of Snow White's good fortune. She flew into a rage and disappeared in a flash of lightning!

Snow White married her prince, and went to live in his castle. The seven dwarfs visited them often, and Snow White and her prince lived happily ever after.